A Very Strange Little Boy

Jim Gratiot

Jordan —

Keep on Reading!

DEDICATION

To Jason William and Jacob Daniel…
always and forever my strange little boys.

TABLE OF CONTENTS

ACKNOWLEDGMENTS

This one's easy—I'd like to give a heartfelt thank you to every single person who has taken the time to actually read one of my books. To the teachers who have read it to their classes, to the parents who have read it to their kids at night… and especially to the kids who have read it just because it looked like a good story. I'd also like to thank my family for giving me tons of great material to use in these books, and for being my cheerleaders when I didn't want to finish. Finally, a special thank you to Becca, my old friend and new editor, who steered me in the right direction on several occasions.

And, once again, a special thank you to Ron Leishman (www.toonclipart.com) for providing a great image for the cover.

PRINCIPAL JONES

Josephine Jones had been principal of Roosevelt Elementary School for 23 years—and during that entire time, nobody had *ever* seen her smile. The students whispered that she had an ugly face and an uglier soul.

Principal Jones was a large, clumsy woman who wore several pounds of cheap, jingling jewelry around her thick wrists. She had a fleshy, wart-filled face that had given more than one student a screaming, wet-the-bed nightmare.

When she spoke it was in a loud, harsh voice—to prove she didn't tolerate *a single ounce of nonsense* from anybody.

Not from her teachers… not from those pesky parents who were always begging for special favors for their kids… and *especially* not from the students themselves.

"This school would run just fine," she liked to say, "if it weren't for all the darn students."

Josephine Jones liked to be called "Jo-Jo" by her close friends. But the teachers at Roosevelt liked to joke (quietly, of course, and far behind her back) that she could count the number of people who actually called her "Jo-Jo" on one hand and still have a few fingers left over.

During the past 23 years, Principal Jones had seen her fair share of juicy scandals—the kind that caused bloody ulcers to develop inside her enormous gut. The kind that caused the lumpy black veins on the side of her neck to bulge out like they were trying desperately to escape.

For instance, there was the Great Graffiti Scandal, where an angry fifth-grade girl named Alice Bethany Coates spray-painted naughty four-letter words on the outside of *every single classroom window*. The funny thing was that Alice Bethany Coates was the worst speller at the entire school, so most of her four-letter words actually contained five or six.

When Alice Bethany Coates was told to pack her things and never set foot on the Roosevelt campus again, her mother said something about Principal Jones that grew into a school legend: "She'll expel you just as soon as look at you."

Three years later came the Grotesque Garbage Scandal, where two extremely bored sixth-grade twins collected their family's stinkiest garbage in their tree house for three months, then spread it around every inch of their classroom. They claimed they did it because their teacher, musty old Larry Landon, had given them detention for no reason at all (although in fact they had poured half an inch of glue on his chair when he wasn't looking).

The putrid garbage stink lingered in the classroom for several months, but the twins weren't around to smell it—Principal Jones had them both whisked away to juvenile hall for the rest of the year.

The strangest scandal of all was the Pathetic PTA Protest, where a dozen Roosevelt parents burst into a crowded PTA meeting, waving hand-painted signs and singing "We Shall Overcome" in loud, off-key voices.

For some reason they thought this would convince the PTA that the school library needed more books. But all it really did was convince everyone in town that the parents at Roosevelt Elementary School were complete lunatics.

Principal Jones made sure none of those parents ever attended a school function again.

When all was said and done, these scandals had one thing in common—Principal Jones CRUSHED them quickly and without an ounce of pity. She left those responsible cowering, or crying, or both—and when they pleaded for mercy or begged for forgiveness, Principal Jones gave them neither.

For 23 years, Josephine Jones ran Roosevelt Elementary School *her way*—with an iron fist inside an iron glove.

But then, during her 24th year, something happened that she wasn't able to crush. Although it started innocently enough, it eventually became so huge it threatened to destroy Principal Jones *and* her precious school.

It started with a phone call.

Principal Jones answered the phone on the fourth ring. She *never* answered on the first ring because she thought it made her look weak.

The mother on the other end was extremely upset, practically blubbering into the telephone. (Principal Jones referred to parents like these as "hysterical bozos.")

"Principal Jones," the mother cried. "Kendall told me he was playing handball at recess like he always does... just minding his own business... when this g-g-girl popped out of nowhere and k-k-kissed him on the mouth. She attacked him! And Kendall was just playing handball. You know, minding his own business!"

"You told me that," Principal Jones said. "Twice. But let me tell you, calling me about something this unimportant is without a doubt the STUPIDEST waste of time I can imagine!"

"But she *kissed* him," Kendall's mother insisted. "On the mouth!"

"Oh, the horrors will never end," Principal Jones mocked. She smiled wearily and slammed down the phone. She glared at it for a moment, almost *daring* it to ring—but she knew she had made her point, and that Kendall's worrywart mother wouldn't be calling back anytime soon.

Kissing? *Oh, the horrors*, she had said.

Yes, kissing. But strong, powerful Jo-Jo, absolute ruler of Roosevelt Elementary School, had no idea that for her the horrors were, in fact, just beginning.

THE TATER TOT TUSSLE

Kendall Curley was practically a handball machine—not only was he the best player in the third grade, he could beat most of the fourth and fifth graders at Roosevelt as well.

Although he was shorter than most of his classmates, Kendall had amazingly quick feet, powerful shoulders, and jaguar-like quickness. There was no ball he couldn't run down, and when he swung his hardest, the ball would sail 30 feet over his opponent's head, where they'd watch in frustration as it landed on the grass with a loud, hollow thump.

On the handball court, Kendall Curley was a maniac.

Off the handball court, however, Kendall was the opposite—pleasantly soft-spoken and almost shy. He might even be considered ordinary, the kind of boy who could stand in a room for 20 minutes before you noticed he was there.

As a result, he didn't have many friends—but fortunately he hadn't made any enemies either.

That is, until one fateful Wednesday in May when he made a strange little first grader very, very angry.

Wednesday at Roosevelt Elementary School was hot lunch day. Students were served gourmet delicacies like pepperoni pizza, fried chicken, cheeseburgers, and tater tots.

While the pizza and chicken and cheeseburgers were generally well liked, there wasn't a single student at Roosevelt who didn't *love* tater tot day.

On non-hot-lunch days, students threw away most of their lunches—it wasn't unusual to see entire untouched peanut butter sandwiches, whole apples and carrot sticks, and even half-eaten cookies piling up in the garbage cans. So much healthy food was thrown away that the PTA held a yearly assembly to talk about what an awful waste of food it was.

But it was a rare Wednesday when you could look into a garbage can and find even a single tater tot lying at the bottom of it.

The first, second, and third grade classes ate lunch together at a circle of decaying wooden tables called The Grove. Other than the occasional food fight and some minor name calling, these lunches usually occurred without incident. After all, the faster everybody finished their lunches, the faster they would be excused to play.

On tater tot day, the students lingered a few minutes longer than usual. There were two reasons for this—the first, obviously, was that those deep-fried rolls of goodness were the cream of the hot lunch crop, infinitely better than the greasy pizza or fatty chicken. The second reason was that tater tots came with little ketchup packets, and there were few things more fun than jumping down on a pile of these packets, trying to spray globs of ketchup in your classmates' hair.

Some Wednesdays, it wasn't unusual to see half a dozen students running around the playground with ketchup clumped into their hair. But it was all in good fun—nobody complained, not even the girls, as long as the school kept serving up those tater tots.

The funniest kid in the third grade was a portly, quick-tongued boy named Terry O'Hennesey. On this particular Wednesday Terry wasn't feeling well, so he shouted high above the lunchtime chatter: "I'm full… anybody want my tater tots?"

There was a brief moment of silence.

Followed by chaos, almost panic, as 40 second- and third-grade students made a mad rush toward where Terry was sitting.

Kendall Curley, who happened to be eating at the next table, bolted out of his seat and was the first to grab Terry's plate (or so he thought). The kids sitting around him were impressed—although not surprised—by his quickness.

Even Terry, who would be sent home later that day with a 103 degree fever, couldn't help but smile. He made a dramatic sweeping gesture to Kendall with his hands, as if he were relinquishing a priceless treasure to a rugged adventurer.

The moment Kendall touched the plate, his ears were shattered by the wail of a tiny first grader he hadn't even seen. He was sprawled on the ground near the tip of Kendall's sneakers.

"Those were *my* tater tots!" wailed the first grader.

"Sorry… but I got them first," Kendall said.

"You cut in front of me," the small boy insisted. "You knocked me down!"

"I didn't even see you," Kendall said.

"Yes you did!" the boy screamed. "Everybody saw you. THIEF!! You're a thief and a bully and you're stealing *my* tater tots."

Tears were running down his cheeks; his normally pale face had turned three shades of purple. He continued howling for over a minute, then turned and stomped back to the first-grade table like a spoiled child who'd been denied a candy bar.

The other third graders began to laugh—who did this little clown think he was, demanding food from an older student? That was against the school code. It simply wasn't done.

Besides, Kendall had clearly gotten to Terry's plate first.

So Kendall, without thinking much about it, took Terry's precious tater tots, popped them in his mouth like they were candy, and went back to sit at his table.

That, it turned out, was a *huge* mistake.

On Monday the following week, Kendall was having another typically brilliant day at handball. He had destroyed nine straight challengers at the morning recess, eleven at lunch, and eight more in the afternoon.

Minutes before the final recess bell rang, Kendall was locked in an intense match (for him) with a fourth-grade girl named Ingrid Swanson. Her nickname was "Popeye," because her enormous arms and shoulders allowed her to crush a handball almost as far as Kendall.

But it didn't really matter—Kendall was so dominant that the ball seemed to float toward him in slow motion, allowing him to set his body and *smash* the ball against the wall.

Popeye pounded one last towering hit. The ball sailed high into the air—Kendall's eyes drifted up toward the ball, squinting slightly into the sun. He cocked his elbows and tightened his fists, ready to put Popeye out of her misery.

As the ball drifted down, however (still apparently in slow motion), something unexpected happened. A pair of tiny hands grabbed Kendall's ears and yanked his head downward. The rubber ball bounced off the top of his head with a dull thud and rolled over onto the grass. Kendall had no idea what was happening, but when he looked down he found himself face to face with an extremely pretty first-grade girl with dimples in her cheeks and venom in her eyes.

"This one's for Simeon, you tot-stealing moron!" she said.

Then she kissed him, twice, directly on the mouth. Right there on the handball court, in front of the entire school.

The kids who were lined up at the handball court burst into nervous laughter, but Kendall couldn't see them—his eyes immediately swam upwards against his forehead, and everything went dark...

A VERY STRANGE LITTLE BOY

There was no denying that Simeon McAllister was a strange little boy—a strange little boy who didn't like having his tater tots stolen.

In all fairness, however, it must be said that he was not the *only* strange member of his family.

Simeon was the only child of Monroe and Elizabeth McAllister, the richest couple in town. They lived on a hill in a sprawling three-story Victorian mansion. They had painted the top story red, the middle story white, and the bottom story blue. The locals called it the Flag House—and it was indeed every bit as ugly as it sounds.

Monroe McAllister earned his fortune by breeding rare, exotic spotted ferrets. People flew to him from all four corners of the earth—and paid several thousand dollars each—to buy these beautiful and feisty creatures.

Monroe was a short, stocky man with mutton-chop sideburns and a larger-than-life personality—when he walked into a room, you *knew* he walked into the room. He wore outrageous cowboy hats and held up his pants with a shiny solid-gold belt buckle in the shape of a ferret. Even the license plate on his convertible 1966 Mustang spelled out FRTBRDR, although Simeon insisted that some people might read this as "Fart Brother Doctor," whatever that meant.

Monroe's wife, Elizabeth, stood out in a crowd for a very different reason—she was nearly seven feet tall, with bulging marble-blue eyes and an impossibly long neck. Elizabeth ran a chain of nine successful tattoo parlors (inherited from her father) called *Ink or Swim*. She was as quiet as her husband was loud. Other than her giraffe-like neck, the main thing people found odd was that although she was responsible for 99% of the tattoos in town, she herself didn't have a single one.

But it wasn't just because of his parents that Simeon was considered strange. They were free thinkers, after all, and encouraged their only son to live his life the way *he* wanted to live it.

As a result, Simeon had developed several peculiar habits he was proud to call his very own.

Why exactly did people consider Simeon McAllister so strange?

They considered him strange because he boasted a huge collection of dead insects—cockroaches, Jamaican crickets, millipedes, and fire ants, to name a few. He kept them all neatly named and labeled right below the cold cuts in his mother's industrial-size freezer in the kitchen.

They considered him strange because he could recite the entire works of William Shakespeare from beginning to end, but couldn't name a single baseball or football team.

They considered him strange because he blurted out random jokes at completely inappropriate times in class—so often that his normally mild-mannered teacher, Mrs. Lawrie, had resorted to throwing large pieces of blackboard chalk in his direction. (This didn't stop Simeon from telling his jokes, but it sure made Mrs. Lawrie feel better.)

And they considered him strange because in that loud, nasty world known as Roosevelt Elementary School Simeon, and Simeon alone, was known as *King of the Cootie Kissers.*

This is how it happened…

During his very first week of first grade, while his classmates lined up for handball, or played foursquare, or simply sat and nervously watched the bigger kids play, Simeon kept busy digging in the dirt for bugs. And he found plenty of them—red ants, potato bugs, and even an orange-colored beetle he was able to add to his collection.

He considered these lunchtimes time well spent.

In the odd moments when he wasn't busy digging, Simeon watched his classmates play—however, perhaps because he was an only child, Simeon didn't have an overwhelming desire to play with them. He was content simply to watch—and as he did, something struck him as unusual.

Simeon noticed that several of the girls on the playground (including some from his own class) spent their entire lunch periods chasing after the boys. Furthermore, being the perceptive boy he was, it only took him until the second week of first grade to realize that *these girls NEVER actually caught any of the boys.*

The whole thing seemed ridiculously stupid.

But Simeon was curious—if you were a girl, why would you spend your energy running after somebody you knew you couldn't catch? And if you were a boy, why would you spend your energy running away from somebody who couldn't catch you?

So Simeon, who had an unusually intense desire to know how the world worked, decided to ask.

"It's more fun than collecting acorns," one of the girls told him, her nose held high with self-righteous logic.

"I like to see their eyes get big when I get close," another said. "I'm waiting for the day one of them pees his pants."

"It's just what girls do," another said. "My mom told me she used to chase after boys… and her mom said that *she* used to chase after boys."

The boys, of course, had a different point of view.

"Girls are mutants," one said. "They have tiny brains and nothing better to do than chase after us."

"I don't try and figure it out," another said. "But when some crazy pony-tailed girl comes after me puckering her lips… I RUN."

After he had asked a dozen of the older, wiser kids—mostly been-around-the-block third and fourth graders—Simeon hadn't changed his opinion.

The whole thing *still* seemed ridiculously stupid.

But Simeon had learned that some things in life simply didn't make sense. Some things *just were*. And there were enough worthwhile things in the world that *did* make sense to waste time worrying about the things that didn't.

So Simeon decided not to worry any more about it.

And he *didn't* worry any more about it—not until the awful Wednesday when that rude third-grader Kendall Curley stole the tater tots that were rightfully his. Discouraged and embarrassed, Simeon stomped off knowing he couldn't fight Kendall physically—but after thinking about it for a while, it occurred to him that there were certain students at Roosevelt who *would* be able to fight Kendall.

So Simeon, with a slickness that even the most successful salesman would have appreciated, approached the prettiest girl in his class and made her an offer—a hoard of junk jewelry and candy—she simply couldn't refuse.

Nina Norfingen was not only the prettiest girl in the first grade, but the quickest as well. This lethal combination made Nina one of the cootie kissers the boys feared the most.

She grinned from ear to ear when Simeon laid out a blanket full of treasure before her.

"I need you to do me a favor," Simeon told her, with a confidence that was slightly unsettling in a 7-year-old. "I want you to chase the boys like you always do… but then I need you to take it one step further."

Nina fingered a crinkly bag of golf ball-sized gumballs and looked at Simeon intently.

"Whatever it takes to get me all this amazing stuff," she said.

Simeon had to keep himself from laughing—this was going to be *easy*.

"All you need to do is keep chasing the boys like you always do," Simeon began. "Except for the one they call Kendall Curley…"

Nina looked thoughtful, as if she had heard the name, but couldn't quite place his face. (In truth she knew his face well—she was friends with one of Kendall's sisters.)

"What about Kendall?" Nina said.

"The rest of the boys you're going to chase," Simeon said. "But Kendall you're going to *catch*."

Catch? Nina looked momentarily shocked, as if she had never considered anything so outrageous.

"One kiss… on the lips," Simeon announced, with the flair of a circus ringmaster. "And all this will be yours."

The next Monday, Kendall lay sprawled and confused on the handball court. Popeye and fifty other students formed a semi-circle around his body, not wanting to touch him. Nina, the warrior, had kissed him quickly, then disappeared to collect her loot.

Rumors began to spread immediately, like they only can on a school playground. By the time school started the next morning, Kendall Curley was a pitied victim, Nina Norfingen was a girl not only to be feared but respected, and Simeon McAllister, that strange little boy with the bug collection, officially became known as *King of the Cootie Kissers*.

KING OF THE COWARDS

Principal Jones sat at her desk, softly gnawing on an onion, garlic, and liverwurst sandwich—she would easily have won the prize for Most Disgusting Breath Ever by a School Principal. She was trying hard to tune out the annoying chatter of the students playing outside. The sounds of the playground were familiar enough—the screeching and yelling, the constant scuffing of tennis shoes, the rough hollow bounce of the red rubber balls—but they still made the thick hair on the back of her neck stand on end.

Principal Jones slipped off her shoes and propped her sweaty bare feet on the edge of her impossibly clean desk—she had a strong dislike of clutter. Grey stringy pieces of lint dusted down from her stubby toes like dirty snow.

She rubbed the moist soles of her feet with her hands, yawning so loudly that she didn't hear the first knock at the door. The knocking grew louder, eventually growing into a pound. Principal Jones bristled and quickly put her feet back on the floor. She scowled at the door, knowing the news behind it would be bad. She had instructed everybody at the school, students and teachers and parents alike, that unless aliens actually landed in the middle of the soccer field, she was in no way, shape, or form allowed to be interrupted during lunch.

Lunch was *her* time—to relax her mind, her body, and her aching, lint-covered feet.

When Principal Jones opened the door, she was met by the terrified sunken eyes of Mr. Blount, her gruff, hunchbacked assistant principal. His enormous nostrils wheezed open and shut, ruffling the greasy black hair that grew like weeds out of them. He clenched down on his dentures so hard his lips disappeared into his mouth.

Students liked to joke that Mr. Blount was older than the dinosaurs—and that he had begun working at Roosevelt about the time the Cro-Magnons discovered fire. This was ridiculous, of course—Mr. Blount had been a teacher and assistant principal for a mere 57 years and had, in grand style, celebrated his 78th birthday just a few days earlier.

"What is it this time?" Principal Jones barked, before Mr. Blount had even entered the room. "A paper clip war? A littering contest? An exploding toilet?"

Among the many things Principal Jones disliked on this earth, her least favorite was cowards. And Mr. Blount was, in her mind, the King of the Cowards. He got scared disciplining students… he got nervous delivering bad news to parents…

and worst of all, he had a greasy, groveling way of informing Principal Jones about every idiotic and unimportant problem that came his way.

Mr. Blount managed a weak smile.

"Josephine," he said. "Things are getting out of control out there."

"Nonsense!" Principal Jones insisted, putting on her most terrifying face. "Things don't get out of control at *my* school."

Mr. Blount slowly opened his hand.

When Principal Jones saw what he was holding, she was struck by an emotion she hadn't felt in 24 years—*fear.*

Before today, Principal Jones had not considered the situation to be at a crisis level. However, she *had* noticed that ever since Kendall Curley had been "attacked" (to use his hysterical mother's overly-dramatic word) on the handball court, the girls seemed to be chasing the boys with more purpose than usual. They weren't any faster, of course, but there was now a very deliberate method to their madness.

Principal Jones found the whole thing slightly troubling, although she couldn't have told you why. However, she decided that as long as none of the other parents called to complain, everything would be just fine.

While there *was* indeed a method to the girls' madness, what Principal Jones didn't yet know was that little Simeon McAllister was the one behind it.

21

In the days following the Kendall Curley Incident Simeon—with help from Nina Norfingen—recruited seven other girls to be in his cootie kissing army.

Each morning before the school bell rang, Simeon conducted that day's "battle plan," tossing out candy and treats and jewelry as he walked the girls through the plan for the day. Usually the victim was a boy who had done something to Simeon—cut in line or laughed at something he was wearing, that sort of thing—but sometimes Simeon picked a boy just because he didn't like his looks or the way he talked.

It only took about two weeks for Simeon McAllister to become the most feared person at Roosevelt Elementary School.

Other than Principal Jones, of course.

Minutes before Mr. Blount opened the door and ruined Principal Jones' lunch, he stood at his post at the far end of the basketball court, sternly monitoring the playground.

For a 78-year-old, he had a keen sense of sight, and was usually quick to spot signs of trouble. That being said, the chaos of the playground didn't bother him like it did Principal Jones—after all, girls had been chasing boys every day of the 57 years he had worked at the school. He had simply gotten used to it.

Today, however, Mr. Blount heard a disturbing scuffle somewhere over by the slide. He moved quickly, trying to catch the troublemakers in the act, but he was a few seconds too late.

As Mr. Blount approached, a pudgy fourth grader named Alex Exhart appeared from behind the ladder of the slide. He was disoriented and glassy-eyed, and his entire skin was covered with… something red.

Alex limped over to Mr. Blount, muttering nonsense. He tossed something at Mr. Blount's feet, mumbled a few more words, and collapsed to his knees.

Mr. Blount managed to escort Alex to the school nurse before timidly walking back to the office to explain the bad news to Principal Jones—that the girls were now *completely* out of control.

Principal Jones crossed the floor, her bare feet squishing into the carpet. She grabbed the thing from Mr. Blount's open hand and sneered at it.

It was a bright red lipstick—the same lipstick that had covered poor Alex Exhart from head to toe.

Principal Jones threw it across the room, so hard it nearly crashed through the window.

"You're a useless wart of an assistant principal," Principal Jones shouted. "But if you do one useful thing here for the rest of your life, I want you to bring me the girl responsible for this!"

She walked over to the tube of lipstick and cracked it with her bare heel. It was just a single tube, sure, but she knew that if this sort of thing was allowed to invade her school, it might eventually get out of hand.

And that, she told herself, could NOT be allowed to happen.

THE BEAUTIFUL NINA NORFINGEN

Veronica Novotny considered it both a blessing and a curse to have an older sister like Ellie.

Ellie Novotny, who was two years older than Veronica, was a cool, ridiculously stylish girl with enormous dimples and curly blonde hair that fell almost to the back of her knees. Most of the boys in her class were in love with her.

Like many sisters, Ellie and Veronica didn't get along. They fought about anything and everything. Their squabbling began the minute they woke up in the morning and didn't finish until their parents sent them off to bed.

But their constant fighting was only part of the problem.

The other parts of the curse were equally annoying to Veronica—having to wait forever to use the bathroom in the morning, seldom experiencing the thrill of wearing *new* clothes (Veronica practically lived in Ellie's hand-me-downs), and never being asked to tag along on excursions to the movies or the mall.

On the other hand, there was one huge blessing that came with having an older sister like Ellie—getting to watch the revolving door of ultra-popular friends who always seemed to be hanging around their house. Veronica was usually excluded from their actual conversations (after all, who wanted to talk with a *baby?*), but she became skilled at eavesdropping from around the corner, and listened every opportunity she could.

As a result, by the time she entered kindergarten, Veronica knew more than most girls about the things that really mattered in life—clothes, makeup, how to wear the latest fashions and, most importantly, boys. Of course she also learned some icky things as well, like the best way to kiss a boy (although this *would* come in handy a few years later).

Two weeks before kindergarten, Veronica was lounging on the couch, drinking a can of apple juice and drawing a picture of an elephant. Her sister crashed gracelessly through the front screen door like she always did, followed by two of the most beautiful girls Veronica had ever seen. One was tall and the other was short. Ellie and the short girl didn't even look at her as they ran straight up the stairs.

The tall girl, however, didn't walk immediately up after them. She had the dashing look of a movie star, the graceful poise of a ballerina, and the aloof confidence of a fashion model—all rolled into one.

She walked over to Veronica and, without saying a word, grabbed Veronica's picture and took a good long look at it.

For a moment Veronica thought she was going to tear it in half.

"That's the most awesome elephant I've ever seen," the girl said instead. "What's your name?"

Veronica didn't know what to say. "V-V-Veronica," she said.

"I'm Nina," the girl said. "Nina Norfingen."

"I can't draw nearly that well," she continued. "You're really talented."

Veronica beamed.

"Well," Nina said with a wink. "I'd better go upstairs now. I'm sure I'm missing some exciting conversation about boys."

"Bye," Veronica said.

Nina bounded up the stairs to Ellie's room. Veronica watched her go. Then she walked slowly up to her own room, glowing with pride.

Veronica tacked the elephant picture on her wall and plopped down on her bed. Having one of Ellie's friends actually talk to her felt better than eating three helpings of double chocolate ice cream.

When I grow up, Veronica told herself, I'm going to be just like her.

When Veronica entered kindergarten at Roosevelt Elementary School, she was thrilled to discover she could watch Nina Norfingen, her new hero, in action every single day. Sure, her class was separated from the big kids by a rusted chain-link fence, but that didn't stop Veronica from having a front row seat to the daily drama that took place on the playground.

While her classmates were digging in the sand with cheap plastic trucks, playing princess over by the concrete tunnel, and playing intense games of freeze tag, Veronica would stand wide-eyed by the fence, watching Nina skillfully chase the boys around the playground. Some days she actually caught a boy and kissed him, leaving him mopey and droopy and defeated. On these days, Nina would march back to class with a look of extreme confidence—a look that Veronica wanted for herself.

It didn't take long for Veronica to decide that when she finally escaped that chain-linked prison next year, she was going to become a cootie kisser, just like Nina was.

For a girl her age, Veronica had a long attention span. Most girls would have watched Nina for a few days, then moved on to something else. But not Veronica. Watching Nina every day made her even more determined to become a cootie kisser. And not just any cootie kisser—the best cootie kisser Roosevelt Elementary School had ever seen.

The cootie kissers, and especially Nina, roamed the playground with a grace Veronica envied. But there was something about the entire scene that troubled her—the girls, as skilled as they were, didn't seem to be making their own decisions about who to chase.

When she asked her sister about it, Ellie told her this was because they *weren't* making their own decisions about who to chase.

According to her sister (who had never been a cootie kisser but was friends with most of them), at the beginning of each day, the cootie kissers would get their orders from a peculiar but powerful second grader named Simeon, a rat-faced kid with burning blue eyes, a permanent cowlick directly on the back of his head, and a steady supply of candy and jewelry he handed out from a tie-died bag.

Ellie told her that Simeon sat on his shaded throne of tanbark underneath the slide, barely moving, silently and sneakily handing out instructions for the day. In other words, although he was King of the Cootie Kissers, he didn't really *do* anything.

One day, as she watched her beloved Nina stalk and kiss another victim, Veronica told herself that next year, when she was a big, important first grader, things on the playground were going to change. She didn't know how she was going to do it, but she was going to make that strange little boy go away.

What Veronica didn't know was that Simeon McAllister was King of the Cootie Kissers in name only. The true power behind his throne came from Principal Jones, who did everything she could to make sure Simeon *stayed* in power.

At first, Principal Jones had been annoyed by all the chaos Simeon and the girls created. After a while, however, she realized that Simeon could actually be a huge help to her—by keeping her students in line. Therefore, not only did she mind if Simeon sent his screechy girls out to attack boys on the playground each day, she actively *encouraged it.*

There was just one condition—absolutely NO lipstick.

Principal Jones loved the idea of keeping her students on their toes—as long as she could do it without leaving any proof (and without lipstick, there would be no proof.) All the angry phone calls from parents were met with stiff, angry denials. All the complaints from the boys themselves were simply laughed away.

Principal Jones and Simeon McAllister made a good team. While Simeon gave the orders to the girls, it was Principal Jones who filled his tie-died bag with treats and treasure. It was even Principal Jones who instructed Simeon who, exactly, was supposed to be attacked, er, kissed, each day.

THE LEGEND BEGINS

The kids who lived on Veronica's street ran ragged during the summer—cruising from house to house, raiding refrigerators, messing up yards, playing hide and seek and kick the can. Outside from early morning until the last blip of sunshine disappeared from behind the large oak trees, they made the most of their summer vacation, often having fun until their parents literally had to drag them inside to bed.

The kids who lived on Veronica's street made the most of their summer vacation—everybody except Veronica, that is. While she definitely helped to raid a few well-stocked refrigerators and frolicked in several soothing sprinklers, Veronica spent most of her summer in a full-fledged, maniacal obsession that had only one goal—to knock Simeon off his cootie kissing throne.

Veronica was 100% determined that by the end of the next school year, Simeon McAllister would be a worthless memory, a disgraced King, an insignificant joke. Veronica, seven years old and full of fire, told herself that by the end of first grade *she* was going to rule Roosevelt Elementary School as the all-powerful Queen of the Cootie Kissers.

As summer neared its end, however, Veronica still didn't have a plan—Simeon was simply too powerful, and had too many loyal girls in his cootie kissing army.

Fortunately for her, during the very first week of school, Veronica got help from a completely unexpected source.

It was clear that Simeon hadn't gotten any less strange—or any less arrogant—over the summer. He arrived at school his first day of third grade wearing an oversized black bowler hat and a red t-shirt with the inscription $E = MC^2$, whatever that meant. He walked through the halls with a dangerous swagger, practically daring people to cross his path. And they didn't— not at the lunch tables, not on the way to the bathroom, and especially not out on the playground. Even the youngest kids had heard the whispers in kindergarten—Simeon McAllister was *not* to be messed with.

To prove to the younger kids how powerful he was, Simeon ordered one of his cootie kissers to save his place in line on the very first hot lunch day (pizza, naturally). There were the usual grumblings of "no cuts" and that sort of thing, but of course nobody said anything directly to him or put him in his place. Simeon held his droopy piece of pepperoni pizza up like a trophy, ignoring the outrage of the kids behind him. He had a very obvious smirk on his face.

When he went back to get a second slice, Simeon crossed right through a mass of first graders—they look so small, he thought to himself—and actually knocked one or two over. Simeon laughed—what were they going to do, tell the principal on him? Simeon didn't even look at his tiny victims; he just grabbed another piece of pizza and greedily began to take a bite.

The slice was nearly to his mouth when something solid as a bag of bricks tackled him from behind.

Simeon fell chin-first against the servers' table, and could actually feel one of his front teeth rip out from his gums. He licked blood off of his chin, groggily got to his feet, and turned to face the beast who had the arrogance not only to tackle him, but to knock out one of his teeth.

Simeon stood up and stuck out his chest. Even through his pain he almost laughed—the kid barely came up to his stomach.

He looked hard into the eyes of a sour-mouthed first grader, whose own teeth were clenched so hard that most of the blood had drained from his face.

"You knocked my tooth out, you sprite-sized punk!" Simeon exclaimed.

The first grader stared into Simeon's eyes and did not blink.

"Touching me is a crime around here," Simeon shouted, as the entire school began to gather around them. "And I'm going to make sure *you* get the guillotine."

The first grader frowned slightly—he obviously had no idea what a guillotine was.

Simeon wiped off more blood from his chin.

"I'm going to cut your head off," Simeon explained. "What do you think about that, you sniveling little snot?"

He lifted his fists in front of his face, like boxers did in the olden days. The entire school quickly formed a circle around them—if there was one thing that brought the students of Roosevelt together, it was a good old-fashioned fistfight.

"Take your best shot, you brat!" Simeon shouted. This shout brought the first action from the yard duties, who were achingly slow to respond to trouble.

Mrs. Jensen, the spryest of the two, managed to walk right into the circle (which was completely surrounding the "fighters") just in time to see the first grader rear back, squint his eyes, and punch Simeon McAllister with the force of a sledgehammer, right below the belt.

Simeon immediately saw stars and collapsed to the ground. The students in the circle all gasped at the same time. Mrs. Jensen screamed.

Once Simeon caught his breath (which took several minutes), he bawled like a baby while the first grader slowly looked around the circle. What he saw were a few looks of awe, but many more of fear.

With that one mighty punch, the legend of Simeon McAllister began to fade…

…and the awful legend that would become Stuart Leroy began to grow.

AND THEN THERE WERE ELEVEN

Stuart Leroy's "Punch Heard 'Round the Playground" was exactly the opportunity Veronica was looking for.

Practically overnight, Simeon McAllister went from being the invincible force behind the cootie kissers who terrorized the school, to simply being a strangely dressed third-grader who couldn't defend himself against a kid half his size.

Not only did the students at Roosevelt no longer fear Simeon, most of the cootie kissers in his grade, including Nina Norfingen, completely deserted him. They were now embarrassed even to be seen with him.

Veronica knew that if she truly wanted to become Queen of the Cootie Kissers, she was going to have to find some loyal worker bees to do her dirty work—preferably loyal worker bees who had *not* been in Simeon's army. Veronica wanted fresh blood—a gang of ruthless cootie kissers who would kiss any boy she ordered them to kiss.

She herself would kiss only when absolutely necessary.

Veronica wasn't going to tolerate anybody thinking for herself, either, so she knew she was going to have to choose the girls for her gang *very carefully*. After all, some of them might be skilled at chasing and kissing boys, but would be horrible at taking orders. Other girls might be the opposite—excellent at following Veronica's orders, but useless at actually catching any boys.

The very afternoon after Stuart Leroy's punch, Veronica made a long list of all the girls at Roosevelt who might potentially make good cootie kissers.

She immediately crossed a handful of girls off the list—those who weren't good-looking enough, those who nobody liked, the crybabies, and the thumb-suckers. She crossed off those with older siblings who might interfere with her plans, and a few more who might have the gaul to actually question the orders she gave.

When all was said and done, Veronica had compiled a list of 17 girls. She wrote their names on index cards and tacked them to the pink bulletin board in her bedroom. Over the next few days, Veronica paid a short, private visit to each girl, explaining what she wanted them to do. She let them know what an honor it was to be asked by Veronica herself. She also reminded them that if for some unexplainable reason they *didn't* want to become part of her gang, they had better keep their mouth shut.

Otherwise, they would regret it for the rest of their school lives.

Seven daring girls told Veronica they wanted nothing at all to do with her or her stupid cootie kissing gang. (Although they said it more nicely than that—they could tell that Veronica was completely serious, and didn't want trouble.)

"You couldn't pay me all the money in the world to kiss a boy," one said.

"I'm afraid of the principal," another said.

"My mom would kill me if I got caught," another said.

Veronica didn't try to convince these girls—she just sweetly reminded them that if they weren't brave enough to join her gang, that was their business. But if they betrayed her, or ratted her out, or so much as breathed a word about what she was doing to their parents, their priest, or their principal, Veronica would make them regret it forever.

They believed her. So they all kept their mouths shut.

That left ten girls—girls desperate to be popular and liked, girls who practically swore a blood oath that they would deny being cootie kissers to anybody... especially Principal Jones.

Once she had established her group of loyal soldiers, Veronica knew it was time to pounce. Although Stuart's punch had taken the wind out of Simeon's sails, and although Nina and most of the other third graders now pretended not to even know him, a handful of younger girls still stood by Simeon, and even acted as his bodyguards.

In order to get rid of these stragglers, Veronica knew she was going to have to make one swift, final attack on Simeon McAllister. So she schemed and schemed until she came up with a very simple plan.

Everybody at Roosevelt Elementary School knew that Principal Jones had no tolerance for lipstick. Since the Alex Exhart Incident a couple of years earlier, a few cocky girls had tried to bring it on campus, but they had painfully and tearfully learned their lessons. Two had even been suspended.

Veronica looked at it this way: If only one or two girls brought lipstick to school, Principal Jones could punish them, give them detention, or call their parents. Or worse.

But what if there were so many girls that Principal Jones couldn't possibly catch them all?

Veronica's plan worked even better than she expected— Simeon McAllister's glorious reign as King of the Cootie Kissers ended one Thursday afternoon when he entered the boys' bathroom across from the school office.

The moment he shut the door, a swarm of girls (eleven of them, to be precise) pounced on him—*every one of them wearing bright red lipstick*. It was like the Alex Exhart attack all over again—except this time, instead of being the ringleader of the attack, Simeon McAllister became its well-known victim.

When news of the attack spread throughout school, all the younger cootie kissers immediately deserted Simeon as well. He now couldn't *pay* anybody to take treats from his tie-died bag.

As predicted, Principal Jones went absolutely crazy—but Veronica's quick planning (each girl was given a pocketful of baby wipes, so when they came out of the bathroom their lips were clean) kept Principal Jones from identifying even one of the culprits.

For several weeks afterwards, Principal Jones' horrifying anger brought all cootie kissing to an absolute halt. Combined with Simeon's sudden silence, there became a stern, well-enforced cootie-kissing void at Roosevelt Elementary School.

But eventually, like it always did, Principal Jones' anger subsided—and once the coast was clear, Veronica was finally able to launch her cootie kissers into action.

THE REIGN OF TERROR

Veronica Novotny had a very different style of leadership than Simeon McAllister.

Simeon was a smooth talker who had offered his cootie kissers sugar and shiny things. Veronica, on the other hand, ruled strictly by fear and intimidation. The ten girls who were bold enough to join her cootie kisser army knew that to betray Veronica would result in the worst consequence ever—*never being popular again.*

Veronica was as well-prepared as she was ruthless—beginning with three "golden rules" every one of the cootie kissers was forced to learn, memorize, and live by:

One: When kissing a boy, you must leave *absolutely no trace at all.* This means <u>no lipstick</u> and <u>no witnesses</u>. If a victim is cowardly enough to approach Principal Jones or their parents, they must look like a BIG, FAT LIAR.

Two: If you get caught by an adult, you will TAKE ALL THE BLAME YOURSELF. You will not reveal any secrets of the group. You will not reveal the names of any other member of the group—especially the Queen!

Three: Anybody breaking rule one or two will personally have to answer to Veronica Novotny, and LIFE AS YOU KNOW IT WILL BE OVER FOREVER!

"Just to be clear," Veronica said, when she first announced her rules. "You will get NO second chances with me. If any of you even *thinks* about breaking one of these rules, you'll wish you'd never been born."

"And that," she said, banging her fist loudly on a desk, "is a promise."

Fortunately for Veronica, she had chosen wisely, and not a single one of her cootie kissers ever turned on her. Over the next few years, Veronica and her army attacked 127 boys, and not a single one was able to prove what happened.

Veronica Novotny was an equal opportunity tyrant—meaning she was as cruel to girls as she was to boys. Boys liked to act tough, grunting and tackling each other and telling dirty jokes and showing how far they could kick a stupid football. But boys weren't usually dangerous—most of them were grunting meatheads, incapable of original thought. And they certainly weren't any threat to Veronica or her gang—she merely had to walk within 10 feet of any boy at Roosevelt to see the fear in his eyes, and the eternal question on his brain— *am I the next target?*

While the boys weren't much of a threat to her, the girls were. Any time a girl tried to talk to Veronica, her "mean meter" would click on, and she would send them away with a curse and a snarl. Most of the time they left in tears. Occasionally, if the girl was particularly mousy, Veronica might feel a slight twinge of guilt, but that guilt usually vanished within a minute or two.

Veronica knew that the only way to keep control of her cootie kissers was to keep all the other girls away. And if she had to step on a few fingers or hurt a few feelings along the way—well, that was just the cost of being in power.

A few weeks after Veronica launched her daily reign of terror, Principal Jones got wind of what was happening— whether through rumor or first-hand account, nobody could say. At first she was furious, but something about Veronica intrigued her. Whether it was her cunning or the meticulous way she orchestrated her attacks, Principal Jones found herself feeling an emotion she had never felt toward one of her students in a long, long time—*respect.*

So Principal Jones gave Veronica and her friends freedom to kiss at will—although she was very careful not to let Veronica know that she knew.

Principal Jones believed it was important to keep students on edge—even the exceptional ones.

For nearly three years, until the first few months of fourth grade, Veronica Novotny and her cootie kissers ruled the school.

These eleven girls (ten plus Veronica) eventually became known as *The Cootie Kissing Eleven*. Veronica loved the name—and was proud to be their mean and terrible queen.

In order to cement her power, Veronica made a fourth "unofficial" rule: no existing girl was ever allowed to leave the group, and nobody new was ever allowed to join.

It was the Cootie Kissing *Eleven* for all time, she thought.

And everything was perfect.

That is, until that terrible day when a new girl moved to town—and her name was Darla Delaney.

THE SUPERSTAR

Even at nine years old, Darla Delaney was a sports superstar, and the closest thing Franklin Canyon had to a local celebrity. She was the type of kid old people bragged about in coffee shops—"Yeah, I'm from Franklin Canyon... you know, where Darla Delaney lives."

When she was six, she joined a fast-pitch boys' baseball team. The other team's parents heckled her when she walked to the plate, but when she smacked the first pitch so far over the fence that it smashed through a car windshield, the heckling stopped.

Darla was voted Most Valuable Player that year.

That fall, when she was seven, Darla played soccer for the very first time. Her teammates weren't thrilled when she joined their team, since she had never played before. But after she scored 11 goals in the first two games, they welcomed her with open arms.

Darla was voted Most Valuable Player that year.

In Franklin Canyon, Darla was the golden girl—it didn't matter if it was baseball, or soccer, or lacrosse, or horseshoes, Darla was ALWAYS the best.

Everybody in Franklin Canyon loved Darla, and not just because she was good at sports. She was also a fun-loving, sarcastic firecracker who could make you laugh until your guts hurt. She was friendly and confident and outgoing, too, so she was pretty much the life of any party she was invited to. And she was invited to *lots* of parties.

In other words, Darla was living a pretty perfect life.

Until, just one month after the start of fourth grade, her parents sat her down and, with sad, stern faces, told Darla the worst news she could imagine—*they were moving!*

After throwing a world-class tantrum (she was even good at those), Darla decided to look on the bright side of things. Maybe moving wouldn't be the worst thing in the world. After all, she made friends easily, so she knew *that* wasn't going to be a problem.

Plus, she had pretty much conquered all the sports teams in Franklin Canyon. Now she'd have an opportunity to become a superstar in a brand new town.

Poor kids, she thought with a playful grin, they're not going to know what hit 'em.

Darla Delaney was determined to make the best out of a bad situation. Unfortunately, never in her wildest dreams did she imagine she would meet somebody as rude, vile, and just plain mean as the girl who obviously ruled her new school.

It only took about three minutes for Darla to realize that Veronica Novotny was going to do everything in her considerable power to make sure that Darla never, ever became a superstar at Roosevelt Elementary School.

The fourth-grade teacher, Mrs. Reiner, had attended seven different schools in nine years (her dad was in the Navy), so she knew how hard it was to be the new student. Without knowing she was lighting a stick of dynamite, she asked Veronica—who had an almost super-human power of making teachers think she was the sweetest girl ever—to show Darla around the school on her first day.

"The first impression is the most important," Mrs. Reiner reminded Veronica. "So please do everything you can to make Darla's first day a memorable one."

"It'll be memorable all right," Veronica cooed, putting Mrs. Reiner immediately at ease.

Darla and Veronica knew immediately they were NOT going to be best friends.

For starters, Veronica wore her most fashionable fuzzy pink sweater... while Darla wore her favorite San Francisco Giants sweatshirt.

Veronica wore stylish black stretch pants… while Darla wore comfortable blue jeans.

Veronica wore adorable pink shoes with brass buckles… while Darla wore shiny new tennis shoes.

Veronica completed her outfit with a jaunty red beret on her head… while Darla wore a Baltimore Orioles baseball cap on hers.

Veronica, through gritted teeth, couldn't help but comment.

"It's your first day of school," she said, just seconds after meeting the new girl. "Why aren't you dressed up?"

Darla frowned. "Who cares what day it is?" she said. "I dress to be comfortable, not to impress anybody else."

"It shows," Veronica said. "But don't you care about making a good first impression?"

"Nope," Darla said. "I only care about making an *honest* one."

"Hmmm," Veronica said, leading Darla toward the bathroom (the first and most important stop on the where-things-are-at-Roosevelt tour).

"Hmmm, what?" Darla said. This prissy girl looked like she wouldn't last three seconds in a game of tackle football. In fact, she looked like she had probably never even *played* a game of tackle football, because she might break a nail.

"Nothing at all," Veronica said, smiling widely and regaining her composure. "I'll just let my 'hmmm' speak for itself."

"It's going to be a long year," Darla muttered under her breath.

"What was that?" Veronica said.

"You heard me," Darla said.

The two girls locked eyes, hatred growing by the second. Darla wasn't particularly worried—she knew that in a one-on-one fight she would turn Veronica into her own personal rag doll. What she didn't know was that Veronica had an army of strong, obedient girls behind her. Girls who would do *anything* she asked them to do.

In other words, with Veronica there was no such thing as one on one. There was only *one on eleven* —which was a huge obstacle, no matter how strong and confident you were.

In the next several months, Darla Delaney found this out the hard way.

A VERY LONG YEAR

In December, Veronica decided to throw an extravagant Christmas party at her house. Like a ruthless dictator trying to impress all the little people, she invited everybody in her class, just so they would know how loving and caring she really was.

One cold morning when Mrs. Reiner darted out for a potty break, Veronica skipped from desk to desk, passing out elegant envelopes that had calligraphy writing on the front and a stylish green and red ribbon around the center.

"One for you," she said, handing an invitation to a tough-looking brown-haired boy. "And one for you," she continued, floating an envelope onto the desk of a startled girl who had never, in three years, even *talked* to Veronica Novotny. The girl handled her invitation delicately, as if it were made of glass. Or diamonds.

Veronica delivered her invitations, one by one. Then, making sure that Mrs. Reiner hadn't finished her business, she stopped in front of Darla's desk.

She stuck her hand in her bag, loudly pretending to search for an invitation that wasn't there.

"Oh, how sad," she cooed, sticking her face mere inches from Darla's. "All my invitations seem to be gone. I guess that means you'll just have to stay home that night and CRY."

Darla could hear the laughter in the classroom building, but she still managed to look Veronica directly in the eye. She was about half a second away from ripping that pretty turned-up nose directly off Veronica's face. Veronica's nose was saved, fortunately for her, when Mrs. Reiner walked back into the room.

"Settle down, everybody. Take your seats," Mrs. Reiner said.

Veronica took her seat, but not before giving Darla a searing look that felt like a knife through her heart. Darla managed to hold it together until recess. The moment that recess bell rang, however, she was the first one out of her seat. She just barely made it to the bathroom stall before bursting into tears.

Darla was a very proud girl. She didn't cry easily and rarely got angry. Unfortunately, several other things happened during the next couple of months that made her not only want to cry, but to tear Veronica Novotny's head off.

For instance, one day the Cootie Kissing Eleven stole all the food out of her backpack—including two slices of her mother's incredible homemade sausage lasagna—and replaced it with a foot-long trout that had been decaying for at least a week.

A few weeks later, Darla was using the bathroom when somebody tossed several water balloons into her stall. The balloons were filled with permanent green ink that ruined her favorite sweater.

One muggy Friday afternoon, four members of the Cootie Kissing Eleven accosted her on the playground (well out of sight of Mr. Blount and the other yard duties). They had stolen several chalkboard erasers and pounded them in Darla's face until she was literally gasping for breath.

The very worst was during the Winter concert. Somebody tripped Darla right as she was walking onto stage, bloodying her chin and nose in front of 500 horrified parents, including her own.

Not only was Darla physically tormented on almost a daily basis—usually subtle things like gum in her hair or a tack on her seat—but Veronica spread a series of lies that made the boys and girls in her class not only hate Darla, but think she was mentally unstable.

For instance, Veronica told everybody she saw Darla walking home from school, picking her nose with both arms in up to her elbows.

She told everybody that Darla's dad was not really a lawyer (as Darla insisted), but a dirty bum who traveled on rat-infested trains and got his family's food out of trash cans.

And she told everybody she had seen Darla kissing Eddy Coletrane one afternoon at the park. For some reason this one upset Darla the most.

Even worse than the rumors was the intentional silence. Veronica gave the Cootie Kissing Eleven strict instructions that they were not allowed, under ANY circumstances, to say a single word to Darla Delaney. If she tried to speak to them, they were ordered to turn up their noses and walk away.

By the time Valentine's Day rolled around, Darla Delaney was easily the most picked on student at Roosevelt Elementary School—all because one snotty girl didn't like the way she looked.

As if *that* daily torment weren't enough, Darla found herself dealing with an enemy even more dangerous than the Cootie Kissing Eleven.

Stuart Leroy.

Although he picked on everybody at school, Darla's turn came one rainy Saturday when he forced her to eat raw snails. Rather than feeling sorry for her, however, the Cootie Kissing Eleven and her other classmates simply made fun of her even more.

Every night after that, Darla fell asleep staring at her ceiling, wrestling with an emotion she'd never felt in Franklin Canyon—an obsessive desire to get revenge on Veronica Novotny.

Her days, on the other hand, were spent worrying about what brutal thing Stuart was planning to do to her next— because once Stuart struck a victim, he generally kept on striking them.

Darla tried to enlist the help of Eddy, Charlie, and Brian, Stuart's favorite victims, but they were more interested in making fun of Darla than they were in protecting themselves from Stuart.

If she was going to get out of this mess, Darla told herself, she was going to have to do it alone.

THE SNAKE & THE PORCUPINE

One Tuesday, Stuart Leroy sent Darla a hurtful note that asked the ugly question: DO ALL THE GIRLS AT SCHOOL HATE YOU???

Of course, this stung because all the girls at school *did* seem to hate her.

Stuart sent mean notes to Eddy, Brian, and Charlie as well—so naturally, at morning recess they huddled together to discuss what they were going to *do* about the situation. As they were talking, Veronica and two of her friends walked by, smirking, holding their noses, and making rude kissing noises.

Darla was tempted to jump up and separate Veronica from a few of her perfect white teeth, but she stopped suddenly—because somewhere deep inside of her, a seed of an idea began to grow. That afternoon in class, as she dully sat listening to Mrs. Reiner drone on and on about poetry, that seed blossomed into a full-fledged *tree* of an idea.

Later that day, something even more amazing happened.

As Darla was riding her bike to Mr. Cooper's (*alone*, as usual) to buy candy, she was struck by an invisible bolt of lightning—an inspiration that nearly knocked her off her bicycle.

Darla stopped pedaling right in the middle of the sidewalk. She picked the last piece of bubble gum out of her hair (that was the Cootie Kissing Eleven's sticky weapon of choice, lately), and decided, right then and there, *that she had had enough!*

It stops today, she told herself—all of it!

The teasing… the gossip… being tripped, kicked, and spit upon. Everything stops—the gum in the hair, the eraser dust, the notes taped to her backpack.

Everything.

Darla often envisioned Veronica as a snake—a bright-eyed cobra wearing a pretty pink bow, but with sharp, dagger-like teeth full of poison.

Darla knew the best way to kill a snake was to cut off its head. Unfortunately, Darla had spent most of her energy the past several weeks fighting against Stuart, that nasty, snail-serving, egg-throwing, mean-note-writing bully.

Darla and her friends (if indeed Brian, Eddy, and Charlie could be called friends) had even started a club, the Defeat Stuart Leroy Club (DSLC, for short). She considered this the only way to stop the bullying.

But so far, the DSLC hadn't defeated much of anything.

If Veronica was a snake, then Stuart was a snarl-faced porcupine, full of deadly quills. No matter which way he brushed against you, you were apt to get poked.

Darla imagined herself holding a knife in one hand, having to decide how to kill the snake and the porcupine at the same time. But Darla knew it was futile—if she attacked the snake, the porcupine would sneak up and stick her full of quills.

On the other hand, if she attacked the porcupine, she'd end up dead or crippled from a snake bite.

It was an unfair fight, two against one. Each of her opponents was strong, in their own way, and of course it was impossible to attack both of them together.

Unless…

Darla stood on the corner, a bike handle in one hand and a box of Junior Mints in the other. Her mind swirled.

Snake. Porcupine. Snake. Porcupine.

Unless…

And then it hit her. Why did she have to attack the snake and porcupine separately?

What if she used the *snake* to attack the porcupine. Or vice versa.

Darla poured the remaining Junior Mints down her throat, then got on her bike and rode home, her brilliant, evil plan becoming crystal clear in her mind.

As luck would have it, a perfect opportunity to implement her plan presented itself that Friday. Well, perhaps it wasn't *entirely* luck—Darla had been secretly watching Veronica from the moment the last school bell rang.

Veronica didn't leave school immediately, of course. She loitered on the playground for 20 minutes or so, laughing and gossiping (and no doubt plotting) with the other members of the Cootie Kissing Eleven. Eventually, the girls clustered around her went their separate ways, and Veronica was left alone.

Veronica rode her bike to Mr. Cooper's (like so many kids did), and picked out several lollipops before riding to the mostly-empty park. Although it was a beautiful afternoon, the only people there were two chatty moms pushing their kids on the swings and a group of older men playing soccer on the field.

Veronica parked her bike and walked over to the slide. She pulled a towel out of her backpack and spread it carefully out on the sand. Then she pulled out a dog-eared Judy Blume book, a can of 7-Up, and a sour apple lollipop.

Veronica sat down on her towel. When she took a sip of her drink and began to read, Darla got off her bike and tiptoed very slowly and quietly to where Veronica was sitting.

Darla was amused to see that Veronica Novotny moved her lips when she read—she actually said the words out loud as she was reading them, like she was telling a bedtime story to an invisible friend.

Darla didn't pounce at once—that would have been too easy. But as she watched Veronica sitting on that towel without a care in the world, she suddenly realized that the only reason Veronica usually seemed so invincible was that *she was always surrounded by lots of people.*

Safety in numbers.

But now, alone, Veronica was like a snake that had forgotten its fangs. And, thought Darla with a cruel smile, it's *much* easier to kill a snake that doesn't have its fangs.

Darla moved closer, until she was so close behind her she could almost feel Veronica's hair rustling in the warm breeze.

"Hey slimeball," Darla growled. "I need to talk to you." Darla's voice was rough and forceful, like a chainsaw. Veronica jumped three feet in the air. Before she knew it, the book was grabbed from her hands and the lollipop ripped from her mouth. She herself was pushed off her towel into the sand.

Darla threw the book and lollipop as far across the park as she could. Veronica looked into Darla's eyes and saw a completely different girl than the one she tormented every day at school. The one *who never fought back.*

Even in her fear and confusion, one very clear thought crossed Veronica's mind: *I'm in BIG trouble.*

But to her surprise, Darla didn't attack her (although she *did* threaten to stuff the lollipop up Veronica's nose)—instead, she asked her for a favor. Veronica had no choice but to listen.

"I'm going to make this simple," Darla began, as soon as she was sure she had Veronica's complete attention. "You're going to help me—you and those horrible friends of yours."

Veronica barely even blinked. She couldn't remember the last time she had been so frightened.

"We don't have to like each other," Darla said. "But if we don't bond together, Stuart Leroy is going to tear us both apart. Of course he'll destroy me first, 'cause I'm by myself. I'm an easy target.

"But one of these days Stuart's going to want a challenge—and you guys are the biggest challenge there is. And one of these days when you least expect it, I guarantee he's going to make you and your stupid friends wish you'd never been born.

"And," Darla said, with half a smile on her face. "if he doesn't attack you soon, *I'm* going to make you wish you'd never been born.

"So we can either be friends," Darla continued. "Or we can fake it so well that everybody *thinks* we're friends. I don't care either way. But starting right now, today, you're going to call your girls off of *me*... and you're going to focus their energy on Stuart instead."

Veronica finally blinked.

"Do what you have to do... call whoever you need to call... but I need you guys to make Stuart Leroy the most miserable wretch EVER to walk this earth."

When Darla explained the evil plan she had in mind, Veronica burst out laughing.

"I didn't think you had it in you," Veronica said. "Maybe we will be friends after all."

Darla walked over and gave Veronica back her book. As they rode to Mr. Cooper's to buy Veronica a new lollipop, Darla thought that maybe, just maybe, Veronica was right.

FOUR MEAN GIRLS

Ten nervous girls sat in a semi-circle in the middle of the soccer field, staring eagerly up at their beloved leader.

Veronica had called an emergency meeting of the Cootie Kissing Eleven at morning recess. To make sure they wouldn't be overheard, she decided to meet as far away from the playground as they could without old Mr. Blount getting them in trouble.

Veronica cleared her throat.

"I have a very good reason for what I'm about to say," Veronica began. "But nobody is allowed to ask me what that reason is."

There were a few murmurs from the Eleven, but Veronica put her hands up and the girls were quiet again.

"As of today, Darla Delaney is no longer our enemy, and we will no longer do *anything* to her. If I hear of anybody even looking at her funny, you'll have to answer to me."

More murmurs.

"You will treat Darla like a friend," Veronica said. "No matter how hard that might be for some of us.

"Instead, we're going to focus ALL our attention on Stuart Leroy—beginning right now. He is our greatest threat, and unless we destroy him soon, he's going to destroy us first.

"And we're NOT going to let him do that to us."

Veronica paused for a moment, to let her words sink in.

"Any questions?" Veronica asked.

There were a few whispers here and there—but Veronica was their queen, so whatever questions or thoughts they might have had, the girls smartly kept them to themselves.

During their talk at the park, Darla had told Veronica exactly what she wanted the Cootie Kissing Eleven to do.

The problem was, eleven girls versus Stuart Leroy didn't guarantee victory—and Veronica knew that if they failed, life as they knew it would be over.

Life as *she* knew it would be over.

Veronica racked her brain, but couldn't come up with a sure-fire solution. Finally, when she was at her complete wit's end, she did what she swore she would never, ever do.

She went to her older sister for advice.

Ellie was blunt.

"You think you're pretty special, scaring all those poor boys," Ellie said. "I'll tell you a secret, though: you might be the almighty queen bee at Roosevelt, but if you stepped onto any other school campus, you'd be just a regular old girl.

"You know why?" Ellie continued. "Because every single school has somebody *exactly* like you—smart and pretty and evil. You rule Roosevelt, but they rule their schools."

Ellie looked Veronica directly in the eyes.

"All you have to do is find these girls, and together you can rule the world."

Then Ellie told Veronica she had tons of homework and slammed the bedroom door in her face. Veronica didn't care. By the time she fell asleep that night, she knew exactly what she had to do.

The next day at school, Veronica once again gathered together the Cootie Kissing Eleven. Between soccer teams, karate classes, gymnastics, and older siblings, it took less than five minutes to learn the names of the cootie kissing queens at the three other elementary schools in town.

After finding their addresses in the local phone book, Veronica invited each of them to a gathering with a very convincing gold-lined invitation that read:

To My Fellow Cootie-Kissers:

My school is in <u>desperate</u> need of your help!

Only you—one skilled in the art of cootie kissing— can help!

Please attend a <u>super-confidential</u> meeting at my house this Saturday night (7 pm).

Excellent food and drink (& candy) will be provided!

Thank you for helping us with our struggle. I promise if you are ever in trouble like we are now, we'll be right by your side ready to help.

Veronica Novotny

That Saturday night, four pretty girls sat around a table elegantly decorated with a perfectly ironed pink tablecloth. At each setting was an individual pepperoni pizza, a delectable glass of iced lemonade, and a bowl of green M&M candies for dessert.

Veronica Novotny was, of course, the hostess of this small but extremely important get-together. Each of the other three girls had read Veronica's invitation with a sense of pride and duty. They were cootie kissers, after all—and one of their own needed their help.

Until this evening, none of the girls had met each other before. But they bonded quickly, laughing and plotting and giggling until all hours of the night.

It didn't hurt that all four girls were very much alike—specifically, they were extremely mean, almost without consciences at all.

Bryelle Jorgenson, for instance, had earlier that week stuck out her foot and tripped a girl who was blindly carrying a heavy box of textbooks. The girl dropped the box and skinned both knees, but Bryelle just walked away laughing.

Sabrina Dorchester was the kind of girl who looked sweet and pretty and shy—she would put her arm around your shoulder and comfort you in your time of need. But then, once you had cried your eyes out, she would walk away and tell all your deepest secrets to her friends.

Rhonda Meyers was the worst. She would walk all the way across town, in a pounding snowstorm at midnight, just to tell the loneliest girl at her school that she was NOT invited to her birthday party.

Veronica had the table's complete attention as she described the disgusting boy named Stuart Leroy who was, she assured them, nastier and meaner than *anybody* they had ever met.

No matter how monstrous he was, however, all four girls were confident that by the time next Saturday was over, Stuart Leroy was going to wish he had never been born.

Veronica stared solemnly at the other three girls at the table. She cleared her throat, stood up straight, and wrapped up her speech with a mighty flourish.

"Between now and Saturday I want you to gather together only your strongest girls," she said, after giving them a blow-by-blow detail of exactly what she needed them to do. "No weaklings allowed."

"We'll meet at the park at 8:00 in the morning, ready to go," she concluded.

The other three girls nodded.

"Here's to cootie kissers… and to ruling the world!" Veronica said with a grin.

She raised her glass high in the air.

Bryelle, Sabrina, and Rhonda raised their glasses as well, then they all clinked them together in one smooth, confident, arrogant stroke.

THE BATTLE

On the day of the Cootie Kisser Convention, Veronica Novotny thought of everything.

She arrived early at the stone tables at Piers Park with five-dozen donuts and three enormous thermos' full of hot chocolate. This was Veronica's big moment, and she knew it was important for her fellow cootie kissers to be properly fed.

Before making their half-mile trek to the baseball diamond, Veronica walked the girls through her plan three more times. She hadn't become a world-class cootie kisser by making things up as she went along.

Before they could even see the baseball diamond, Veronica and the cootie kissers could *feel* the uneasiness of the crowd.

Word of the big showdown between Eddy Coletrane and Stuart Leroy had of course spread like wildfire—passing in hushed tones from class to class, from school to school, even from town to town. It was talked about in bathroom stalls, on school busses, and on school playgrounds. (Nearly every single

68

kid wanted to see Stuart get what he deserved—but most people were convinced that Eddy was not going to leave the baseball diamond alive.)

As a result, the bleachers were overflowing—apparently every single kid in town (and several from the neighboring towns) had shown up for the big event.

Veronica could tell by the unsettled murmur that the crowd didn't have any idea what was going to happen. Personally, Veronica didn't really care what was going to happen. All she cared about was hearing the signal, the shrill whistle she and Darla had rehearsed again and again and again.

Everything hinged on Veronica being able to hear that whistle. Because if Darla blew her whistle and nobody came to the rescue—well, it would be like a drowning boy calling for help and Superman flying the other way.

Veronica led the cootie kissers to the first-base side of the baseball field, just behind the dugout. She then directed half of them (with Sabrina as their leader) to their designated spot behind the outfield wall.

As a group they looked rather strange—35 girls (34 plus Veronica) with perfectly-combed hair, beautiful smiles, and pounds of glittery red lipstick—but they didn't cause any commotion because the kids in the stands were too busy watching the drama on the field itself.

The girls took their places.

Standing completely still behind the first-base dugout, Veronica held up three fingers on her right hand—the signal for absolute quiet. A calm came over her. She had taught these girls well, and was confident that each one would do *exactly* what she was supposed to do.

The crowd in the bleachers grew louder and more restless. Veronica could hear Stuart Leroy's muffled voice shout out something unkind.

Then she heard another sound—the unmistakable crack of a baseball bat. Even Veronica, who could barely tell the difference between a baseball and a football, knew the sound meant that somebody—she assumed it was Stuart—had hit the ball really, really far.

Veronica held up one finger this time. The girls paced nervously and silently—the battle was about to start. Veronica kept her finger up for twenty seconds… thirty seconds… forty seconds.

Then came Darla's whistle.

Veronica smiled and clenched her fist—the signal to attack.

Like the well-trained soldiers they were, Veronica and the cootie kissers charged onto the field with eager squeals. The girls behind the outfield wall joined them. Stuart and his friends—and all the spectators as well— were instantly deafened by the viscious war-cry of 35 screeching girls.

The attack went quickly—and it went perfectly.

First, Veronica and the cootie kissers circled their victims like sharks. Veronica looked into Stuart's eyes and saw, probably for the first time ever, real fear. His two friends, who were wimpier versions of Stuart himself, simply looked confused.

The cootie kissers circled the boys until Veronica gave her own well-rehearsed cry. The girls charged immediately, ignoring the terrified pleas of the three boys. The boys tried to bury their heads in the dust, and Stuart even tried to grab his baseball bat and swat the girls away. Veronica, in her absolute glory, grabbed his weapon and heaved it over the backstop.

The crowd went crazy. They didn't know exactly what was happening—there was too much dust to see much of anything—but they had a hopeful sense that Stuart was *finally* getting paid back for all the evil things he had done to most of them.

Eight minutes went by.

Veronica caught a glimpse of Stuart's face through the cloud of choking dust and knew they had been successful. She gave another whistle, and like a cloud that breaks to reveal the sunshine, the girls sprinted off the baseball diamond as fast as they had arrived. They kept running until they reached Piers Park.

Veronica was the only girl who stayed behind, and then only long enough to shake Darla's hand—she had definitely deserved that. When she shook it, Veronica had the odd sense that sometime in the future, she and Darla were destined to be true friends.

She couldn't tell if Darla felt the same way, but that was a problem for another day.

When Veronica finally arrived back at the park, all the cootie kissers cheered and clapped as she walked up to greet them.

"We did good, girls," she shouted. "Pizza's on me!"

So, as morning turned to afternoon, Veronica and 34 dusty cootie kissers went to Frank's Original Deep Dish to celebrate a job very well done.

TWO GLORIOUS WEEKS

For two glorious weeks after the Cootie Kisser Convention, Stuart Leroy did not go to school.

As a result, the number of beatings, stolen lunches, nuclear wedgies, and slashed bicycle tires was cut drastically. Students who usually walked around Roosevelt with timid, horrified looks on their faces suddenly walked through the corridors with confident, bright-eyed smiles.

Even the teachers noticed a difference. Instead of their students wondering what imaginative tortures Stuart was planning for them after school, they were able, for once, to concentrate on their schoolwork.

Immediately after the Cootie Kisser Convention ended, the entire crowd cleared away from the baseball diamond as quickly as possible—because although everybody enjoyed seeing Stuart Leroy delirious and flailing in the dirt at home plate, nobody wanted to be around when he "woke up." That would be like poking the Incredible Hulk with a stick when he was sleeping.

As it turned out, they didn't need to hurry. Stuart and his friends stayed on the ground for nearly three hours. When they finally gathered enough strength to stand up, Stuart said just one thing to his friends, straight and to the point.

"We are NEVER going to talk about this again!"

Stuart limped angrily home, images of revenge already beginning to swirl around in his head.

When Stuart arrived home early that evening, his fawning mother could tell immediately that something was wrong. She could see it in his eyes.

"Oh, my poor Steeeewie!" she cried. "What's the matter with you?"

Stuart brushed right by her. "Nothing," he mumbled. "I'm sick."

Without another word he stomped upstairs to his bedroom, slammed the door, and crawled under his covers, still in his shoes and dusty clothes.

His mother immediately called the school and left a message that her precious baby was sick, and that he probably wouldn't be in for a couple of days. She faithfully checked on him every hour on the hour, and brought him chicken noodle soup and crackers and ginger ale. She sang his favorite lullabies and rubbed his back until Stuart finally closed his eyes.

Then, as soon as she left, he would open them again. Stuart knew that until he had planned his revenge, he wouldn't be able to sleep at all.

After three days of constant, smothering attention from his mother, Stuart told her to stop checking on him. "Leave me alone to sleep," he said. "Just put a cup of soup by the door."

With a sad heart (because her angel was sick, not because he was rude to her), Mrs. Leroy closed his door and went down the stairs, sighing with each step. Poor, sick Stewie, she thought. Mrs. Leroy loved her smart, charming, good-looking, popular son, and she would do ANYTHING in the world for him. So if he said not to go into his room and to just leave a cup of soup outside his door, she would make him the very best cup of soup in the world and leave it outside his door. Just like he said.

Anything at all for her precious baby.

Stuart locked his bedroom door.

He dug through the mound of dirty, stinky laundry that seemed to be growing larger on his floor, until he found a yellow pad of paper. He rummaged through his messy underwear drawer to find a pencil.

Stuart put the pad on his lap and chewed on the end of the pencil, as thoughtfully as he could.

At the top of the page he wrote, in huge letters, the word REVENGE.

Under that he wrote DARLA DELANEY.

He skipped a few lines.

Under that he wrote VERONICA NOVOTNY.

He underlined her name. Twice.

Stuart put the pad on the floor next to his bed, then curled under his covers and managed, finally, to fall asleep.

He woke up two hours later with an evil smile on his face.

Stuart quickly grabbed the yellow pad and pencil, tapped the name "Veronica Novotny" with an eraser a few times, and began to write.

A few minutes later he heard his mother place another bowl of soup next to his door—but, like the obedient mother she was, she didn't even try and come into his bedroom.

Stuart sniffed into the air. The soup smelled great, but it would have to wait.

Stuart kept scribbling on the pad until his Ultimate Plan for Revenge was complete. After that he wolfed down his soup and slept like a baby.

THE FURIOUS PRINCIPAL JONES

Principal Jones was having a good day. After all, the sun was shining, she had an enormous beef and bean burrito waiting for her in the refrigerator, and not a single idiotic parent had called to complain about anything. It was nearly 11:00 in the afternoon, practically a record.

Of course, just as she was thinking these thoughts, somebody knocked at the door. It was a quiet, almost timid knock—well, she thought, it can't be Mr. Blount. He usually knocked with all the grace of a hungry pig eating from a trough of slop.

Principal Jones wiped a spot of drool from her chin (she was thinking about that delicious burrito just a little bit too much) and walked toward the door. She almost didn't answer it—she knew instinctively that the person on the other side would be the bearer of bad news. But of course it might be even worse if she didn't answer it at all.

She opened the door and was surprised to see a sixth-grade boy she hadn't spoken to in nearly three years—Simeon McAllister.

Simeon had grown at least two feet taller since the last time they spoke, but he seemed no less strange. He was disturbingly thin, with a gaunt, humorless face out of which gleamed perfectly round blue eyes that seemed to notice everything. One half of his head was shaved completely bald. On the other side, his stringy hair was dyed neon green.

Since the day long ago that Stuart Leroy had punched him, Simeon had become practically invisible, seldom playing with his classmates, and in fact seldom talking at all. Instead, he devoured science fiction novels at lunch, so quickly that he practically read a new one each day. He would sit at the tables the entire lunch period, absorbed in his latest book about outer space.

If he took any interest in the cootie kisser queen who had replaced him, he didn't show it at all.

Most of his classmates didn't know it, but in the past few years, Simeon had acquired a handful of new and bizarre hobbies—some even more strange (at least to kids) than collecting bugs. For instance, he had amassed a collection of over 500 opera records. It was the only music he listened to, and the rumor was that he blasted these records from the minute he got home until the minute he fell asleep at night. His parents, of course, thought his taste in music was wonderful—

so instead of squashing it, they patiently went about their daily business wearing matching sets of earplugs.

Simeon had also become obsessed with painting—although the only thing he would paint, over and over and over, was a picture of a window on a rainy day. His parents, of course, didn't think this was odd or depressing—they were just glad their son was taking an interest in the arts.

So yes, Simeon McAllister was still strange—and although he didn't show it, he *had* taken an interest in the cootie kissing queen who had replaced him. He wasn't obsessive about it like he was with his books or his opera or his rain-streaked window—but in the back of his mind he knew that if he ever had the opportunity to pay Veronica back for what she did (the attack in the bathroom that had sealed his fate), he would take it in a heartbeat.

Needless to say, the Cootie Kisser Convention was *exactly* the opportunity Simeon had been waiting for.

"Can I come in for a moment?" Simeon asked Principal Jones. "I don't want anybody to see me here."

Principal Jones groaned and let him in, even though he was severely cutting into her burrito time. She began to drool again.

"You have one minute," Principal Jones said, looking at her wristwatch. "Starting now."

"Something happened last weekend," Simeon blurted out. "And I don't think you're going to be very happy about it."

He handed Principal Jones a manila envelope.

"What is this?" she asked.

"This is your worst nightmare," Simeon said. "And mine."

Then Simeon laughed deep in his throat, turned on his heels, and disappeared out the door.

The pictures made Principal Jones so angry she completely forgot about the burrito in the refrigerator. The pictures told the whole story of the Cootie Kisser Convention—the crowd, the setup by Eddy and Darla, and the result: Stuart swimming in the dust and Veronica Novotny gloating over him.

In between listening to opera records and reading science fiction books, it seemed that Simeon had become quite a talented photographer as well.

Principal Jones was furious, although she wasn't entirely sure why. She had tolerated Veronica and her gang for several years, but something about this was just... wrong. Perhaps because it happened away from Principal Jones' precious school and without her knowledge. Perhaps because it was such an unfair fight—30 or 40 against three.

Perhaps it was all the lipstick. Principal Jones *hated* lipstick.

Or perhaps it was because it proved that things had, as Mr. Blount once predicted, finally gotten out of hand.

Principal Jones addressed the school over the intercom—short and to the point.

"Attention Roosevelt students," she said briskly. "Beginning immediately, any student who kisses another student will be EXPELLED immediately. There will be no second chances, and no exceptions. That is all."

As the words faded into the air, Veronica Novotny, who certainly wasn't expecting *that*, blushed nine shades of red as every eye in the classroom slowly turned toward her. She tried to slink down in her seat, but there was absolutely nowhere to hide.

THE END OF THE ROAD

For the first time in 10 years, Principal Jones patrolled the school playground *herself.*

She wasn't going to take any chances with that lazy Mr. Blount, or those useless old hags Miss Thomas and Mrs. Jensen. If there was any funny business happening on her playground, SHE was going to be the one to find out. And SHE was going to be the one who personally signed the expulsion papers.

The normally carefree students of Roosevelt were instantly transformed into nervous wrecks—especially the members of the Cootie Kissing Eleven, most of whom wouldn't walk within twenty feet of a boy, in case Principal Jones mistakenly thought she was chasing him.

Groups of three or more quickly dissolved whenever Principal Jones walked by. She didn't even have to say a word out loud—just the steady sweaty squish of her footsteps and her fierce eyes sent chills up and down students' backs. Her icy stare made even the most innocent student feel like they had just shoplifted ten bags of candy from the local grocery store.

Within one week of Principal Jones' announcement—the one that made Veronica turn nine shades of red—every single member of the Cootie Kissing Eleven had deserted her. They each whispered to Veronica as discreetly as possible that they still *liked* her—they just couldn't risk being seen with her.

Especially since Principal Jones seemed to be watching every single step that Veronica took.

Veronica herself didn't know what to think. A few days earlier she had been the most popular girl in the entire town—the girl who made Stuart Leroy disappear, if only for a little while. Kids she'd never met had come up to her at the five-and-dime and told her how amazing it had been to watch the Cootie Kisser Convention in person.

But now she felt like she had the plague. It was like pulling teeth even to get somebody to play hopscotch with her. Every time she approached one of the Cootie Kissing Eleven, they'd look away guiltily and walk away. Veronica didn't know what to do. She understood *why* her friends had abandoned her, but it still made her feel sad.

Veronica, who had spent nearly every moment of her time at Roosevelt being a cootie kisser, or dreaming about being a cootie kisser, suddenly felt like she was floating on a boat without a sail.

She had been a cootie kisser for so long she didn't have any idea how *not* to be one.

During lunch Veronica, with a heavy heart, would sit down on the wooden rail at the edge of the playground and sadly watch the world go by. Nobody talked to her. Nobody even came near her, for fear that Principal Jones would see them together and get the wrong idea.

After two weeks of being the loneliest girl at the entire school, somebody *finally* came down at lunch and sat down next to her.

"Feels pretty lousy being an outcast, doesn't it?" Darla Delaney asked.

"Worse than lousy," Veronica admitted.

"Well," Darla said. "Now you know how I felt when you guys were making *my* life miserable."

Veronica tried her best to give Darla a reassuring smile.

"Sorry about that," Veronica said. "If I knew how awful it felt, I wouldn't have done it."

"I don't believe that for a second," Darla said with a smile. "I just think you're sorry you got caught."

Veronica didn't know what to say about that.

"But it's okay," Darla reassured her. "My mom taught me I should always forgive people.

"Even if they don't deserve it," she added.

Veronica took a bite of her sandwich and stared into space.

"So I guess I forgive you," Darla said.

"Thanks," Veronica said weakly.

The school bell rang, and both girls stood up to go inside.

"I did want to thank you for the amazing job you guys did last week," Darla said. "You did a favor for everyone, especially me."

"It's what we do," Veronica said. "Or at least it's what we *used* to do."

"Stop feeling sorry for yourself," Darla laughed.

"What else can I do?" Veronica sighed. "None of my friends want anything to do with me."

Darla grabbed Veronica's shoulder so she stopped walking.

"One of your friends does," Darla said.

"Which one?" Veronica asked.

"This one, dummy," Darla laughed, pointing to herself.

Veronica looked her in the eye and laughed herself.

"It's funny how life works out sometimes," Veronica said.

"Sometimes it's funny," Darla said. "And sometimes it's just weird."

"At this point," Veronica said. "I'll settle for a little bit of weird."

The new friends entered their classroom just as the final bell rang. Principal Jones, who had been watching their every movement like a hawk, told herself she was going to have to watch those two *very carefully* from now on.

Then she, too, walked inside.

ABOUT THE AUTHOR

Jim Gratiot is an author, editor, and father of five
perfectly-behaved children and one naughty dog. He
lives with his wife and kids in Folsom, California.

He can be reached by e-mail at
gratiot49@yahoo.com.